LEWIS AND CLARK'S COMPASS

What an Artifact Can Tell Us About the Historic Expedition

by John Micklos Jr.

CAPSTONE PRESS
a capstone imprint

Capstone Captivate published by Capstone Press,
an imprint of Capstone.
1710 Roe Crest Drive
North Mankato, Minnesota 56003
www.capstonepub.com

Library of Congress Cataloging-in-Publication Data is available on the Library of Congress website.

ISBN: 978-1-4966-9578-9 (hardcover)
ISBN: 978-1-4966-9682-3 (paperback)
ISBN: 978-1-9771-5456-9 (ebook pdf)

Summary: In 1803, President Thomas Jefferson doubled the size of the United States with the Louisiana Purchase. He sent Meriwether Lewis and William Clark to lead an expedition, exploring the new land. And one special compass helped them find their way through it all. Find out what made this compass so special and how it earned a place in history.

Image Credits
Alamy: Don Smetzer, 44; Dreamstime: Mkopka, 41; Getty Images: Archive Photos/ Kean Collection, 34, Bettmann, 10, 29, Ed Vebell, 22, GraphicaArtis, 42, MPI, 6; Lewis & Clark Bicentennial © 2004 United States Postal Service®. All Rights Reserved. Used with Permission, cover (back); Library of Congress: 36, Manuscript Division, The Thomas Jefferson Papers, 14; National Gallery of Art: Gift of Thomas Jefferson Coolidge IV in memory of his great-grandfather, Thomas Jefferson Coolidge, his grandfather, Thomas Jefferson Coolidge II, and his father, Thomas Jefferson Coolidge III, 7; National Park Service: Lewis and Clark National Historic Trail, 43, Lewis and Clark National Historical Park, 17 (top), 18; Newscom: VWPics/Greg Vaughn, 12; North Wind Picture Archives: 11, 19, 23, 24, 27, 31; Shutterstock: Ace Diamond, 25, Everett Collection, 4, 5, 15, 26, 33, Olga Popova, 17 (bottom); Smithsonian Institution: 38, National Museum of American History/Mary McCabe, cover (bottom right), 1, 21, 40; Wikimedia: Golbez, 37, William Morris, 9; XNR Productions: 35

Editorial Credits
Editor: Michelle Bisson; Designer: Tracy Davies; Media Researcher: Svetlana Zhurkin; Production Specialist: Tori Abraham

Smithsonian Credits
Barbara Clark Smith, Museum Curator, Division of Political, National Museum of American History; Bethanee Bemis, Museum Specialist, Division of Political History, National Museum of American History

All internet sites appearing in back matter were available and accurate when this book was sent to press.

Printed and bound in China. 4205

TABLE OF CONTENTS

Chapter 1
TRAVELING WEST.................................4

Chapter 2
WHAT A BARGAIN!............................ 8

Chapter 3
HELPING THEM FIND THEIR WAY 16

Chapter 4
EXPLORING VAST NEW LANDS 22

Chapter 5
THE COMPASS KEEPS TRAVELING...............38

Chapter 6
A SYMBOL OF ADVENTURE.........................42

EXPLORE MORE 44
GLOSSARY..46
READ MORE 47
INTERNET SITES 47
INDEX..48

Words in **bold** are in the glossary.

Chapter 1
TRAVELING WEST

William Clark stood outside the wooden walls of Camp Dubois in the Illinois Territory. He walked along the banks of the River Dubois to where it spilled into the mighty Mississippi River. He gazed across the river. In the distance was the mouth of the Missouri River. Clark pulled a silver-plated **compass** from his pocket. He checked the **latitude**. Then he checked the **longitude**. He wrote these figures down in his journal. He noted the date—May 13, 1804.

The next day, Clark and his partner, Meriwether Lewis, would begin a daring journey.

William Clark

The men would lead a group of explorers up the Missouri River. In 1803, the United States had purchased a vast stretch of land in North America from France. Lewis and Clark's team would explore this land. The two-year trip would become one of history's

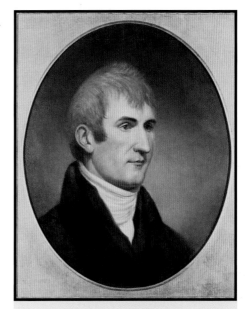

Meriwether Lewis

most famous adventures. The men had no idea what dangers they might find along the way. Whatever they faced, this compass would help guide them.

Latitude and Longitude

During the journey, Lewis and Clark entered many notes called compass **bearings** into their journals. These bearings showed latitude and longitude. Latitude marks a place north or south of the equator. Longitude marks a place east or west of a certain point in England. Together, they can pinpoint any place on Earth. Often, Lewis and Clark linked these bearings to **landmarks**. They might mark a bend in the river or a hill. Clark used the measurements and his descriptions to create maps. These maps later guided other travelers going west.

Lewis and Clark's **expedition** began in 1804. At that time, the United States included just 17 states. Thirteen were the states that had been colonies before the Revolutionary War (1775–1783). Four more had joined since then. All of these states lay east of the Mississippi River. The land purchased from France lay to the west. Many American Indian nations called those lands home. A few white fur trappers had explored some areas. Beyond that, no one in the United States knew what the explorers might find.

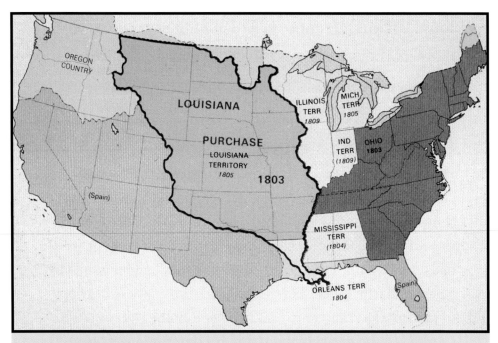

A map of the United States in 1803 shows how the country doubled in size after the Louisiana Purchase.

France had called the land the Louisiana Territory. It stretched west to the Rocky Mountains. It stretched north from the Gulf of Mexico to Canada. Mexico claimed land to the south and west. Several European countries claimed the region that is

President Thomas Jefferson

now Oregon and Washington. All of these countries ignored the fact that American Indians already lived in these lands.

Thomas Jefferson was elected United States President in 1800. He wanted to learn what the lands to the west of the country contained. It wasn't possible, though, because other countries claimed these lands. Then came an opportunity that changed everything.

Chapter 2
WHAT A BARGAIN!

The massive land deal now known as the Louisiana Purchase started with a much smaller idea. President Thomas Jefferson wanted to buy the city of New Orleans from France. This city sat at the mouth of the Mississippi River in the Louisiana Territory. It was a center for trade. Jefferson sent two people to Paris, France, to make the deal. They were prepared to pay up to $10 million (around $225 million today). At the time, French ruler Napoleon Bonaparte was fighting a war with Great Britain. He needed money.

Napoleon proposed a bigger deal. He offered to sell New Orleans and the rest of the Louisiana Territory. The total cost was $15 million (around $338 million today). The United States quickly accepted the offer.

Even today, the Louisiana Purchase stands as one of history's greatest bargains. It included a total of 828,000 square miles (2,144,510 square kilometers).

The price for each acre (0.4 hectare) of land of the Louisiana Purchase was about 3 cents. Today, an average acre of land in the United States sells for more than $3,000. That would make the value of the Louisiana Purchase land nearly $1.6 trillion today!

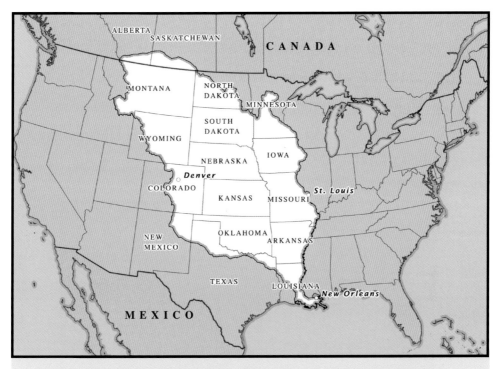

The land in the Louisiana Purchase later formed all or part of 15 different states. These states were: Arkansas, Colorado, Iowa, Kansas, Louisiana, Minnesota, Missouri, Montana, Nebraska, New Mexico, North Dakota, Oklahoma, South Dakota, Texas, and Wyoming.

Jefferson hoped to find a water route to the Pacific Ocean somewhere in the new territory. He referred to it as a Northwest Passage. Such a water route could open up a much quicker trade route to China. At the time, ships sailed from the Atlantic coast. They had to circle more than half the globe to get to China.

Jefferson was eager to know what these new lands held. He had wanted to explore them for years. Now that the United States owned the Louisiana Territory, the explorers would not need to cross areas claimed by other countries.

In the early 1800s, U.S. trade ships traveled from the East Coast all the way around South America to get to China. Finding an internal water route to the Pacific Ocean would mean a much quicker journey.

The explorers would, however, cross the homelands of many American Indians. They had lived there for thousands of years. In the east, the United States had already taken land from American Indians for white settlers to use. Sometimes, American Indians were pressured to sign unfair treaties. Other times, they were removed from their lands by force. The United States wanted to grow. Taking land was part of its **expansion** plan. The United States ignored the rights of the American Indians to their lands.

Colonialism

Leaders of the United States wanted the young nation to get bigger. This involved having white settlers move west. The government believed it had the right to simply take all the land it wanted. Often, the American Indians

American Indians outside a white settlement in Ohio in 1788

who lived on the land were forced to move. Usually, they were moved to poor quality land that no settler would want. This process of taking over and ruling land owned by others is called **colonialism**.

Jefferson needed someone brave and daring to lead the expedition. He knew just who to ask: 29-year-old Meriwether Lewis. Lewis was Jefferson's private secretary. As a former U.S. Army captain, Lewis was a natural leader. He eagerly accepted Jefferson's offer. Lewis wanted a strong partner to join him. He turned to 33-year-old William Clark.

Clark had been an officer in the U.S. Army. He and Lewis had served together. Clark had left the Army in 1796. He managed his family's large farm in Kentucky. He gladly agreed to join the expedition.

A bronze statue called "Explorers at the Portage" shows (from left to right) Clark's enslaved servant York, Clark's dog Seamus, Lewis, and Clark.

Clark's family held about a dozen enslaved people. Enslaved people were treated as property. They were forced to do hard work for no pay. The first enslaved people were kidnapped out of Africa and forced to come to the American colonies. There they were sold. Families were often divided.

A man named York was enslaved on Clark's farm. Clark took him along on the journey. Though he had no choice in whether or not to go on the journey, York played a large role in the trip's success. He hunted for food, helped with American Indian relations, and helped discover new plants and animals.

FACT!
Lewis and Clark shared leadership. Lewis focused more on collecting plant and animal samples. Clark focused more on mapmaking. But they both did whatever was needed at any given time.

Lewis and Clark spent months preparing for their journey. They had one large **keelboat** made. They also purchased two smaller boats. Lewis bought scientific instruments, including the silver-plated pocket compass. He also purchased equipment for setting up camp along the way. The explorers would hunt for food as they went. They carried gifts for the American Indians they would meet. In all, they spent about $2,500 (about $56,000 today) on supplies.

Meriwether Lewis made this list estimating the cost of the goods they would need for their journey.

Lewis and Clark recruited about 45 men to join their team. Some were soldiers. Others were skilled hunters. Some could **navigate** boats. Clark trained the team members for several months, preparing them for the journey.

Finally, in the spring of 1804, the team was ready to depart. They had no idea what dangers they would face during their trip. They did not even know exactly where they were going. But a small, silver-plated compass would help guide them.

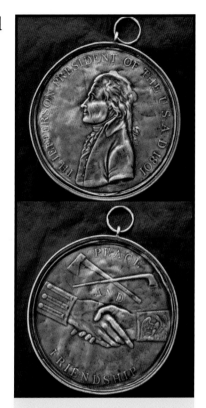

Lewis and Clark gave the Thomas Jefferson Peace Medal to American Indians as a sign of friendship.

FACT!

Thomas Jefferson named the team of explorers the **Corps** of Discovery. He asked the men to keep detailed records of their discoveries. "Your observations are to be taken with great pains and accuracy," he told them.

Chapter 3
HELPING THEM FIND THEIR WAY

Today, finding our way is easy. We simply use the map function on our phone. We type in an address and receive step-by-step directions. Lewis and Clark had no such help as they planned their route. They would follow the Missouri River west to its source. Beyond that, they had no exact plan. They would have no maps to guide them. They would have only simple instruments. The most expensive was a gold-cased timepiece. It told time with great accuracy. This timepiece, used with other tools, would tell them how fast they were traveling.

Lewis and Clark would carry instruments that allowed them to navigate using the stars. Sailors had used such tools for hundreds of years. One key tool was a telescope. They could use this to view stars at night. Perhaps their most important devices were the simplest. The explorers would carry six compasses. One was a silver-plated pocket compass. It became the expedition's most famous **artifact**.

The Corps of Discovery used simple navigating tools compared to the high-tech instruments we have today.

How a Compass Works

A compass detects Earth's magnetic field. This magnetic field has two main poles—the North Pole and the South Pole. The compass has a magnetized needle. It is drawn to Earth's magnetic North Pole. This lets explorers know which direction is north. Knowing this, they can tell which direction they are traveling.

A compass always points to Earth's magnetic North Pole.

Lewis and Clark's journey would take them up rivers. The explorers would travel through dense woods and over mountains. They would use their compasses every day. One compass stayed in the keelboat. This helped them navigate while in the water. On land, they would use a large surveyor's compass to take the bearings of far-off objects. This helped them determine distance and direction. They also carried three smaller brass compasses and the silver-plated compass. All four of these compasses easily fit inside a pocket. The explorers probably used them almost every day.

A surveyor's compass is also called a circumferentor. It is used to measure angles in the land.

Philadelphia was the most populated city in the United States in 1800.

Lewis bought most of his scientific instruments from Thomas Whitney of Philadelphia. Whitney made highly accurate compasses and watches. Lewis knew he needed the finest tools available. There were no maps of the lands his team would explore. These compasses would show them the way. They would guide the explorers across mountains and prairies. The compasses might even save their lives.

Famous Customers

In 1808, Thomas Whitney placed a newspaper ad. In the ad, he said that several famous people had used his compasses. We know that Lewis and Clark were among them. Lewis bought several compasses from Whitney in late 1803. Those compasses traveled with the expedition throughout its entire journey.

The instruments that Lewis and Clark used had to be rugged and sturdy. They also had to be easy to carry. The silver-plated pocket compass met both of those needs. It measured just 3.5 inches (8.9 centimeters) long by 3.5 inches (8.9 cm) wide. It was only 1.5 inches (3.8 cm) thick. It fit easily into a pocket. So did the other small compasses. But the silver-plated compass came in a mahogany box. Mahogany is a hard and durable wood. This compass also had a leather carrying case. The case helped protect it from rain, snow, and dirt.

Historians believe Clark was the one who used this silver-plated compass on the journey. It may have been a gift from Lewis. Both explorers kept journals of the adventure. They used their scientific devices to measure and record their progress. When the trip ended, the explorers sold most of the equipment that had survived. But Clark did not sell the silver-plated compass. He kept it for many years.

The mahogany box and leather carrying case protected the compass from damage on the dangerous journey.

FACT!

Why did Lewis and Clark carry so many compasses? They were afraid that some of the compasses might get lost or damaged during the long journey. Without a compass, they would truly be lost in the wilderness.

Chapter 4
EXPLORING VAST NEW LANDS

On May 14, 1804, the expedition began. Clark and most of the Corps of Discovery left Camp Dubois. Some local people waved goodbye. They must have wondered if the explorers would ever return. Lewis met up with Clark's group about a week later. Then they began the long, difficult journey up the Missouri River.

The Corps of Discovery headed up the Missouri River in their keelboat in May 1804.

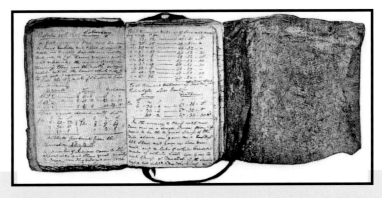

William Clark's diary of their journey survives today.

Moving upriver against the current was difficult. Often, Corps members would pull the keelboat using ropes. They faced rain, heat, and mosquitoes. Lewis, Clark, and other Corps members made many entries in their journals. They recorded their progress. The silver-plated compass and the other tools were constantly in use. For example, on June 5, 1804, Clark wrote down two compass bearings. He reported the Corps had traveled 12.5 miles (20.1 km) that day. That was a good day's travel against the river's current.

FACT!
Both Lewis and Clark kept detailed journals about their travels. These texts allow the public to share in the explorers' adventures.

In August 1804, the Corps met American Indians for the first time. Jefferson had told Lewis to treat each Native nation "in the most friendly . . . manner." The Corps followed his instructions. They handed out gifts at each meeting. Most times, the explorers were greeted warmly. However, the Teton Sioux demanded payment to travel farther upriver. After a few tense moments, the matter was settled peacefully. The Corps continued on its way.

In late October, the Corps reached a large American Indian village in what is now North Dakota. The Mandan and Hidatsa people lived there. Corps members built a fort nearby called Fort Mandan.

A Mandan village in the 1800s

The Corps spent a brutal winter at Fort Mandan. Clark recorded temperatures of minus 40 degrees Fahrenheit (-40 degrees Celsius). He asked the American Indians about what lay ahead. He made rough maps based on their information.

That winter, they met a French fur trapper named Toussaint Charbonneau. They hired him to **interpret** with American Indians. His wife, Sacagawea, became an even greater help.

Sacagawea

Sacagawea was born into the Shoshone Nation. But she was kidnapped by the Hidatsa as a child. She was married to Charbonneau. When Lewis and Clark met her, she was pregnant. She gave birth in February. She and her baby, Jean Baptiste, made the difficult journey with the

A statue of Sacagawea carrying her baby

team. Sacagawea had come from the western lands that lay ahead. She helped guide the explorers. She helped them communicate with the American Indians they met. She was a valued member of the team.

In April 1805, the Corps began moving west again. They knew the hardest parts of the journey lay ahead. Their Mandan and Hidatsa hosts had warned them about huge waterfalls. They had also described steep mountains. Still, nothing could prepare the explorers for seeing these sights in person. Their journals described the awe they felt at coming to the Great Falls of the Missouri River. Their words showed the wonder of seeing the Rocky Mountains in the distance. They described the excitement of seeing grizzly bears and great herds of bison.

Lewis and Clark take a break from their trek while Sacagawea and her family stand behind them.

Lewis and Clark's journals provided important information about western plants and animals. In all, they recorded 122 new animals during their journey. These included prairie dogs, bighorn sheep, grizzly bears, bison, and many types of snakes and birds. They recorded 178 new plants. These included the western red cedar tree, purple coneflower, and more.

William Clark sketched a grouse, a new animal to him. He called it "Cock of the Plains."

These were just the types of discoveries Jefferson had hoped the Corps would make.

FACT!

In the spring of 1805, a group of Corpsmen brought back gifts for President Jefferson. They carried maps, plants, rocks, and examples of American Indian clothing. They even carried a live prairie dog.

On May 26, 1805, Lewis wrote that he "felt a secret pleasure" in having come far enough to see the Rocky Mountains. He added that he saw "sufferings and hardships" ahead. The explorers could not cross these steep mountains in boats. They needed to find horses. Sacagawea said that the Shoshone Nation would have horses. But first, the Corps faced another challenge. On June 2, they reached a fork in the river.

Now the explorers had a big decision to make. Which way should they go? The Hidatsa had told them of the Missouri River and its Great Falls. This river would take them closest to the Columbia River on the other side of the Rockies. That was where the party wanted to go. But which fork led in that direction? A wrong choice could cost them weeks. This might stop them from crossing the mountains before winter. It might even cause the entire expedition to fail. Lewis and Clark took dozens of compass readings. They sent search parties up both forks. There was no clear answer. In the end, Lewis and Clark chose the southern fork. They made the right choice.

Sacagawea helped the Corps of Discovery find their way through land unfamiliar to them.

FACT!

Lewis and Clark let Corps members vote on which fork to take. Everyone except the two leaders thought they should take the northern fork. Lewis and Clark convinced the Corps to take the southern fork.

Two weeks later, the Corps realized they had taken the proper fork. Clark's journal entry from June 17, 1805, described the "deadly sound" of the Great Falls ahead. The explorers were forced to carry the boats and all of their gear around the falls. This process was very difficult. It took far longer than they planned. They had to travel through thick brush. Even worse, on June 29, a flash flood struck. It carried away much of their equipment.

Clark described losing the large compass, an ax, moccasins, and more in the flood. He worried about the compass most of all. "The Compass is a serious loss, as we have no other large one," he wrote. Two men went looking for it the next day. "They found it in the mud and stones," Clark wrote. He must have been relieved. The team needed all of their measuring devices to guide them on this daring journey. The loss of any of them could leave them stranded, lost in the wilderness.

A bison stands on a bluff overlooking the Great Falls of the Missouri River in what is now Montana.

FACT!

It took the Corps nearly six weeks to travel 17 miles (27.4 km) around the Great Falls. This was the slowest part of the entire journey.

The Rocky Mountains loomed ahead. The Corps could not use their boats to cross them. After weeks of searching, they found the Shoshone people. They traded with the Shoshones for horses and food.

In September, the explorers began climbing the mountains. The Corps hiked through deep snow. They ran out of food. They had to eat some of their horses to survive. Finally, they reached the land of the Nez Percé Nation in what is now Idaho. The Nez Percé fed them and helped them make canoes. Soon, the Corps sped down the Columbia River toward the Pacific Ocean.

In November 1805, the Corps reached the Pacific Ocean in what is now Washington State. They had made it! They had not discovered a Northwest Passage. But they had crossed the mighty Rocky Mountains. They had explored new lands. They had completed half their journey. Now all they had to do was find their way home.

Meriwether Lewis takes his first look at the
Rocky Mountains in the distance.

FACT!

The Corps had traveled more than 4,100 miles
(6,598 km) to reach this point. They had
overcome many hardships. Only one person
had died along the way. Sergeant Charles
Floyd died of an illness in August 1804.

The Corps of Discovery built a fort in what is now Oregon. They spent the winter there. On March 23, 1806, they began the journey home. It had taken them a year and a half to travel west. It would take just six months to return. This time, they knew the best routes to take. They stopped to visit with their Nez Percé friends. After crossing the Rocky Mountains, the Corps split up for a while. This gave them a chance to explore some new places.

The Corps of Discovery named their fort in what is now Oregon "Fort Clatsop" after the local Clatsop Indians.

The Corps parted ways with Sacagawea, Toussaint Charbonneau, and their child at Fort Mandan. They were sad to leave them behind. Sacagawea had played a vital role in the journey's success.

Traveling with the current down the Missouri River, the Corps raced home. On September 23, 1806, they reached St. Louis. Townspeople cheered. The Corps had completed one of history's greatest journeys! The silver-plated compass had played a big role. It had helped guide their travels all along the way.

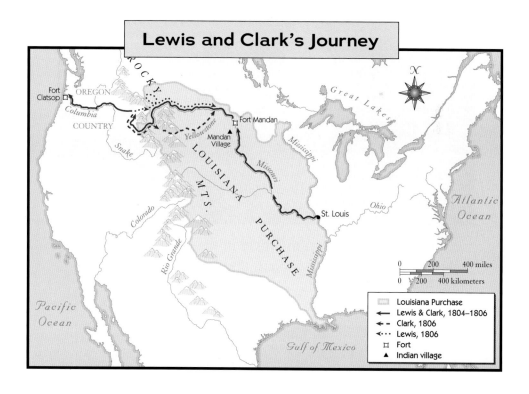

Lewis and Clark's Journey

The Lewis and Clark expedition changed the United States forever. Word spread about the open spaces to the west. Soon, settlers began flocking to these lands. Clark's maps helped guide them. By 1850, the United States had added even more land in the south and west from Mexico. It added the Oregon Territory as well. The United States now stretched from the Atlantic Ocean to the Pacific Ocean.

Americans moved west in droves in the late 1800s. They clashed with American Indians and forced most of them out of their native lands.

As white settlers moved west, American Indians found themselves being pushed out of their native lands. Lewis and Clark had made an effort to make friends with the American Indians they met on their journey. They had received life-saving help from them, including food and horses. Sacagawea guided them much of the way. Without the help of American Indians, Lewis and Clark's expedition would have certainly failed. But the success of their travels had a cruel consequence for American Indians. It led to their homelands being stolen from them.

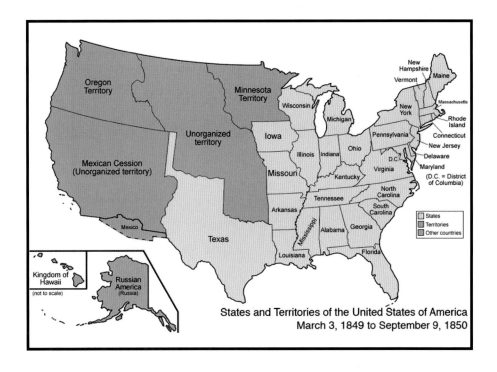

States and Territories of the United States of America
March 3, 1849 to September 9, 1850

Chapter 5
THE COMPASS KEEPS TRAVELING

Only a few items from the Lewis and Clark journey survive today. Some wore out or broke during the trip. Others were lost along the way. Most of the rest were sold. The travelers brought back samples of seeds and plants they had found. They brought back animal skins. Clark brought back maps he had created. These were the items they valued most.

Lewis and Clark scrawled hand-written maps and compass bearings of their locations in their journals.

Once the trip was over, the explorers no longer needed many of the other items. They held a public sale when they returned to St. Louis. People eagerly bought the explorers' gear, such as hatchets, knives, and needles and thread. Some people probably thought these items would make great souvenirs. Others may have thought the items would someday become valuable pieces of history. In all, the sale raised about $400. That is about $8,990 today. The silver-plated compass was not among the items auctioned. Clark kept it.

Lewis and Clark's Journey: Facts and Figures

Total Distance Traveled:	roughly 8,000 miles (12,875 km) round trip
Total Duration:	2 years, 4 months, 10 days
Number of New Animals Recorded:	122
Number of New Plants Recorded:	178
Number of Native Nations Encountered:	around 50

Only one scientific instrument from the journey survives today. That is the silver-plated compass. Clark kept it for many years. It reminded him of his great adventure. Clark served as the first governor of the new Missouri Territory. Later, he was in charge of working with American Indians in the Louisiana Territory. He tried to maintain good relations with the American Indian nations. Often, he traveled to meet their leaders. He probably carried the compass to many of these meetings.

Today the silver-plated compass is part of a Smithsonian exhibit at the National Museum of American History.

The National Museum of American History is in Washington, D.C.

In 1825, Clark attended a treaty meeting at Fort Crawford in Wisconsin. This meeting drew leaders from many American Indian nations. There, Clark finally parted with his compass. He gave it to a friend. The compass remained in the friend's family until 1933. The family then gave it to the Smithsonian Institution. Today, visitors can see it at the National Museum of American History.

Chapter 6
A SYMBOL OF ADVENTURE

The silver-plated compass traveled up and down rivers. It crossed mountains. It traveled roughly 8,000 miles (12,875 km) during nearly two and half years. It helped one of history's greatest expeditions succeed. Without it, Lewis and Clark might not have made it to the Pacific Ocean. They might have died in the snowy mountains. It also helped them find their way back home.

Photography didn't exist during Lewis and Clark's journey, but many artists have recreated scenes from their travels.

Humans have wanted to explore the world since the beginning of time. We have scaled mountains, wandered through deserts, and sailed across oceans. Since the 1950s, we have even begun to explore outer space. Over the years, people have made lists of history's greatest journeys. The Lewis and Clark expedition appears on every list. The silver-plated pocket compass played an important role in that journey. The compass is now more than 200 years old. It remains a symbol of adventure and discovery. But it is also a symbol of the westward movement that forced American Indians from their lands.

The Lewis and Clark Trail

Today, people can sample the route the Corps of Discovery took more than 200 years ago. Visit the Lewis and Clark National Historic Trail. The trail winds for 4,900 miles (7,886 km) through 16 states. It passes many

Visitors stand on Lewis Lookout in Montana.

American Indian lands. Visitors can hike, cycle, and camp through the prairies and mountains that Lewis and Clark saw. They can travel down the Missouri River on rafts or canoes and visit the Lewis and Clark National Historical Park in Oregon.

EXPLORE MORE

A replica of the keelboat Lewis and Clark's team used is displayed at the Lewis and Clark State Historic Site.

Lewis and Clark State Historic Site

Do you want to see the kind of boat that Lewis and Clark used? The Lewis and Clark State Historic Site in Illinois has a full-size **replica**. The wooden boat measures 55 feet (16.7 m) long. The mast stands 30 feet (9.1 m) tall. Imagine traveling in that boat up the mighty Missouri River. That's how life was for the Corps of Discovery in 1804.

Lewis and Clark's Journals

The journals from the journey describe one of history's greatest adventures. They tell what Corps members did from day to day. Journal entries describe the excitement of racing down river rapids. They explain the dangers of crossing the snow-covered Rocky Mountains. The journals tell of meetings with many American Indians. They describe seeing new plants and animals for the first time. Journal entries express the joy of finally reaching the Pacific Ocean. Today, most of the journals are housed at the Academy of Natural Sciences of Drexel University Museum in Philadelphia, Pennsylvania.

Sacagawea Historical State Park

The Sacagawea Historical State Park is located in Washington State. Along with outdoor exhibits and attractions, the Sacagawea Interpretive Center is central to the park. It holds interactive exhibits and sponsors programs that teach about Sacagawea, Lewis and Clark's journey, and the American Indians native to the area.

GLOSSARY

artifact (AHR-tuh-fakt)—an important historical object

bearing (BAYR-ing)—the determination of a position by a compass

colonialism (kuh-LO-nee-al-izm)—taking control of an area and placing settlers there

compass (KUHM-puhs)—an instrument people use to find the direction in which they are traveling; a compass has a needle that points north

corps (KOR)—a group of people doing an activity together, often a military activity

expansion (ek-SPAN-shuhn)—growing, spreading out

expedition (ek-spuh-DIH-shuhn)—a journey with a goal, such as exploring or searching for something

interpret (in-TUR-prit)—to tell others what is said in another language

keelboat (KEEL-boht)—a type of riverboat that is usually rowed, poled, or towed and that is used for freight

landmark (LAND-mahrk)—an object that helps identify a location

latitude (LAT-ih-tood)—the distance measured north or south of the equator

longitude (LON-jih-tood)—the distance of a place east or west of the line north and south passing through Greenwich, England

navigate (NAV-uh-gate)—the science of plotting and following a course from one place to another

replica (REP-luh-kuh)—an exact copy of something

READ MORE

Blashfield, Jean F. *The Amazing Lewis and Clark Expedition.* North Mankato, MN: Capstone Press, 2018.

Llanas, Sheila. *Sacagawea, Meriwether Lewis, and William Clark.* New York: Enslow, 2019.

Micklos, John Jr. *Discovering the West: The Expedition of Lewis and Clark.* North Mankato, MN: Capstone Press, 2015.

INTERNET SITES

Journals of the Lewis & Clark Expedition
lewisandclarkjournals.unl.edu/

Lewis and Clark's Expedition
kids.nationalgeographic.com/explore/history/lewis-and-clark/

The Louisiana Purchase
socialstudiesforkids.com/articles/ushistory/louisianapurchase.htm

Sacagawea
www.historyforkids.net/sacagawea.html

INDEX

American Indians, 6, 7, 11, 13,
    14, 24–25, 27, 37, 40, 41, 43
    Hidatsa, 24, 25, 26, 28
    Mandan, 24, 25, 26
    Nez Percé, 32, 34
    Shoshone, 25, 28, 32
    Teton Sioux, 24

Bonaparte, Napoleon, 8

Camp Dubois, 4, 22
Charbonneau, Toussaint, 25, 35
colonialism, 11
Columbia River, 28, 32
Corps of Discovery, 15, 22–25,
    26, 27, 28, 29, 30, 31, 32, 33,
    34–35, 43

Fort Mandan, 24–25, 35
France, 5, 6, 7, 8

Great Falls, 26, 28, 30, 31

Jefferson, Thomas, 7, 8, 10, 12,
    15, 24, 27
journals, 4, 5, 20, 23, 26, 27,
    28, 30

Lewis and Clark National Historic
    Trail, 43
Lewis and Clark National
    Historical Park, 43
Louisiana Purchase, 5, 8–9
Louisiana Territory, 7, 8, 10, 40

maps, 5, 13, 16, 19, 25, 27, 36, 38
Mississippi River, 4, 6, 8
Missouri River, 4, 5, 16, 22, 26, 28,
    35, 43

New Orleans, 8
Northwest Passage, 10, 32

Pacific Ocean, 10, 32, 36, 42

Revolutionary War, 6
Rocky Mountains, 7, 26, 28, 32, 34

Sacagawea, 25, 28, 35, 37
St. Louis, 35, 39

Whitney, Thomas, 19

York, 13